GULITH
New York

Headhunters Of Nuamerica

Stanton A. Coblentz

ISBN: 978-1-63652-330-9

HEADHUNTERS
OF
NUAMERICA

STANTON A. COBLENTZ

TABLE OF CONTENTS

I

There was a stunned sensation in Downey's head as he slowly regained consciousness. He had the feeling of one who has been drugged, or sandbagged; and for a moment he could not quite recall where he was or what had happened to him. He was only aware of a dull, hammering sound from somewhere in the distance; and aware also of the aching pain and the stiffness in every joint and muscle of his body. It seemed to him at first that his eyelids were glued together, and would never open; and when at length he forced them apart, he realized that he was in darkness, except for a faint light that slowly widened at the further end of a narrow gallery.

A low moan from just ahead of him caused him to reach out; and, more by feeling than by sight, he recognized the slim form sprawled full-length on the floor. Judith Barclay! As this name flashed across his mind, recollection came back with a great leap, and his tortured brain reconstructed the scenes of the last hour or two. The announcement of the outbreak of war, followed almost immediately by the appearance of the raiding planes! His appeal to Judith, when for the twentieth time she had shrugged her thin shoulders and refused him; then the alarm, and their flight together through the panicky crowds toward the air-raid shelters! Their terrified halt, when a bomb plowed up the street just before them; and their dash into an immense section of concrete pipe, where some construction work was under way! And, finally, the thudding sound of a concussion; Judith's scream—and darkness!

"Well, by thunder, that shell pretty near got us!" he reflected, scarcely wondering at the changed appearance of the pipe, which he attributed to the explosion. Then, as he reached out and felt for the girl's arm, he asked, "How are you, Jude? Hurt?"

"No, I'm all right, Mort," she answered, weakly. "Only, a little—a little funny in the head."

He glanced out along the tapering dimness of the pipe, and saw the light at the further end slowly widening. At the same time, the noise of renewed hammering came to his ears. "Well, the rescuers are getting here pretty quick," he remarked. "Guess the raid's over."

"Thank heaven!" she sighed. "I—I don't think this was a very wise place to choose, Mort."

He bit his lip, wondering why, even in their present grim location, her least remark should have the power to torture him.

"Don't you—don't you smell something peculiar? A little like ether?" she went on, in faltering tones; while he, as the light at the end of the gallery brightened to a glare, tottered to his hands and knees, and then fell back to the floor of the tube, feeling sick in the head.

"There's something wrong with the air, by Christopher!" he muttered; and then cried out in astonishment, "Say, do you see that?"

By the bright light at the end of the gallery, two figures were visible. Two men wearing clothes like Scottish kilts, bright crimson and emerald-hued, and with bare arms and knees! Over the lips and nostrils of each was a drooping, scarlet-tubed apparatus, a little like a gas-mask, though different from any gas-mask that Downey had ever seen. And in the hand of the foremost was a minute shining stick, from which suddenly a dazzlingly white searchlight ray shot out, illuminating the two trapped persons as if by a blaze of sunlight.

Downey thought that the strangers started back in surprise; but all that he was certain of was that, after a second, they were motioning him to come out of the tube.

This Downey was able to do only very slowly, while helping the girl, who was tightly clutching at a large beaded handbag. So painful was their progress that the man's mind, still dazed, had little chance to reflect on their rescuers' appearance. Doubtless the strangers were vaudeville performers who, caught by surprise, had had no time to change their costumes.

But when Downey finally came to the end of the tube and stared out, he gasped and staggered, clutched one hand to his forehead, and sank full-length to the ground, in reeling bewilderment.

Surely, the shock had turned his mind! The long marble lines of the Government buildings, which had dominated the scene only a short while before—they were no longer to be seen! The sandstone mansions of Bannerton Row, just to his left, had vanished! He was in the midst of a wide park, featured by gnarled old elms—gnarled old elms a hundred feet high, where there had been not even a sapling!

But if this were only a nightmare, why did Judith share it? For her dazed exclamations showed that her eyes told the same story!

As they breathed the clear air outside the tube, the hazes cleared rapidly from their minds; the strength seemed all at once to course back to their limbs, and they were able to rise to their feet. But each second only added to their befuddlement.

The red-and-green-clad men were but two out of a score. All wore kilted costumes, with bare arms and knees; and all were arrayed in bright colors: purple and gold, chrome yellow, crimson, and milky white. And all had crowded around them with wild exclamations, calling out in high-pitched tones that neither of them could at first understand.

At length, from amid the din, two cries made themselves evident, shrilling in a strange accentuation, "Who are you? Who are you? Where do you come from? Where do you come from?"

To this Downey replied, in a voice that sounded cracked and broken even to his own ears. "Who are *you*? Who are *you*? Where do *you* come from?"

His answer was an outburst of laughter which, beginning in a low ripple, gradually rose to an uproarious crescendo.

This demonstration was checked by the arrival of a tall blue-and-orange-clad individual, who stood out from the others owing to a large gemmed silver star that crowned his bald pate.

Raising his left arm authoritatively, the newcomer instantly silenced the crowd; and, stepping toward Downey and the girl, spoke in slow, crisp tones that were quite understandable despite their foreign ring:

"Better tell us, sir, where you come from. I understand you were both found among the ruins."

"Yes, I guess that's right," Downey replied. "That is, the ruins of the bombing raid."

"Bombing raid?" several voices caught him up, sharply. "Bombing raid?" And the men turned to one another with muttered exclamations; while one or two put their hands significantly to their heads.

"I do not know what you mean, sir," said the star-crowned one. "Must I tell you we are a civilized people, and have had no bombing raids for three hundred years?"

Downey grumbled something beneath his breath, thinking this a poor time for jesting. But incisively over all rose the voice of Judith, "if you have had no bombing raids for three hundred years, then what year is this? Didn't we go through a raid only a little while ago?"

The starred one cast Judith a piercing glance, and replied, contemptuously, "I suppose, then, you're forgotten this is the year 314!"

"That is, 314 by the new reckoning," another voice explained. "2270, if you prefer the Medieval calendar."

Downey and the girl stared at one another, dumbfounded. Could it be that they had slept for more than three centuries?

"Do not forget," the starred one continued, fixing Downey with a severe scowl, "we have yet to account for your presence here. A few days ago, digging among the ruins left by the savages in their war hundreds of years ago, we came across a big concrete tube which, on being opened, gave out fumes that produced temporary unconsciousness in the investigators. Later, as they worked with gas-masks, you two were noticed within. It is evident that you entered sometime after the first opening was made, while the workers lay drugged by the fumes. But where did you come from? That is what we cannot understand."

Downey's mind reeled. An explanation, amazing and yet barely possible, had flashed over him. What if the impact of the explosion had sealed both ends of the concrete tube where he and Judith had sought refuge? What if the tube had been buried beneath the earth, to remain there for centuries? What if the poison gas released by the bombs had entered their retreat, too diluted to kill them and yet strong enough to produce suspended animation? He remembered reading of a new war gas which could cause precisely that effect; and he knew that such substances did exist in nature: as, for example, the paralyzing fluid which the hunting wasp injects into the spider, to keep it indefinitely alive though seemingly lifeless. If such a poison could operate for weeks or months, what was there to prevent it from being effective for a year? for ten years? even for three hundred years?

Then might this not be what had happened to Judith and himself? In their profound unconsciousness, time would have no meaning for them; generation after generation might be born, grow to maturity and old age, and pass away while they slept their dreamless sleep, to be awakened at last when the opening of their tomb had released the poisoned fumes and let in some pure air.

By some swift intuition, Downey felt sure that this was what had happened.

But his new acquaintances were not to be convinced by his explanation. "I do not know where you are from," said the starred one, while his green and orange costume glittered brilliantly in the sun. "You do not talk like natives of our Nuamerica. You know our speech as if from old books, and there is a foreign ring to your voices. Your clothes are strange and clownish—I half believe you have robbed a museum. Either you are foreigners who have no passport, or fugitives who seek an outlandish disguise. For that reason, I proclaim you under arrest! You will come with me to be examined by the High Councillor!"

To the accompaniment of a sound as of rattling chains, three men stepped forth from the crowd. Each drew out a little pistol-like machine, and pressed the trigger; and from the muzzle of each apparatus there shot forth thin shining wires, which, with incredible swiftness, wound themselves about Downey and the girl, binding their arms to their sides beyond possibility of release.

Then, with a brusque "Come!", the starred one stalked away; while the two prisoners, poked and shoved by half a dozen guards, started slowly down an avenue of elms toward the huge triangular doorway of a remote building.

II

As they passed along the tree lined boulevard, their eyes were attracted to several edifices of strange forms and colors. Some were shaped like gigantic mushrooms, and were of a sky-blue complexion; others were like huge inverted sea-green funnels; while the queerest of all was an enormous crystalline sphere that rested on a wide base of black marble. "You see, Jude," Downey remarked, "this is the twenty-third century, sure enough. Was anything like this ever known in our own time?"

"They do look crazy," Judith admitted, "but I'd be crazier yet if I believed what you want me to. We must both be dreaming. That's the simplest explanation."

On reaching the triangular doorway, they passed into a hall whose softly glowing walls were lined with a satiny claret-colored cloth. The floors were of alabaster; the air was rich with pine-incense; and the golden incense burners, upon ebony tables, gave something of the effect of an Oriental temple.

But it was not this that arrested the newcomers' attention. Their eyes were immediately drawn to a figure who, clad in lush crimson, sat on a throne that dangled ten feet above the floor, being suspended from the ceiling by chains. As Downey adjusted himself to the subdued light, he was able to make out that the man was old, very old; his face was seamed and pitted until it might have been mistaken for the mummy of Rameses.

Yet his movements belied his age. He was able to act with the swiftness and decision of youth; and his words, when at length they came forth, were spoken rapidly and with force.

Surrounding him like courtiers, on the floor of the hall, were half a dozen elaborately robed men with faces as creased and scarred as his own. Yet all, despite their appearance of extreme age, moved with an almost youthful robustness; their bodies seemed erect and well developed, with none of the flabby or wizened quality that might have been expected to belong to their years.

It was with a vague discomfort that Downey noted the owlish stares these ancient beings cast at him, nudging one another, and ogling him with unhealthy peeps and squints. In his eyes they were the most repulsive creatures he had ever seen.

Judith, also, appeared to have something of the same feeling. Pressing close, she whispered into his ears, "What is this? The hall of the Harpies?"

The silver-starred dignitary, who had preceded them into the hall, had paused before the suspended throne, and was speaking to the crimson-robed old man, whom he addressed as "High Councillor." Downey could not make out much of his words, but could see how he paused occasionally to point to Judith and himself; and he noted with apprehension the avid gleams in the eyes of the High Councillor, who stared down half curiously, half malevolently at the two prisoners as they stood silently amid the guards.

At length the Councillor motioned the starred one away; beckoned Downey to approach him; and spoke, in the high, piping tones of advanced age:

"Stranger, I do not know where you come from: whether you be a spy from across the ocean, or one who was hidden away by misguided parents in order to escape the Decapitation Draft. In any case—"

"What is the Decapitation Draft?" Downey could not help breaking out.

The Councillor's fist came down angrily, pounding at the vacant air.

"Do not think to save your head," he shrilled, "by pretending ignorance of one of our most honored customs! As I was about to say, unless you can satisfactorily show where you come from, you will be sent to the body-testing rooms; and if you pass, as I believe you will, judging from your sturdy-looking frame, you will be put on the list for early decapitation. Such is the law of Nuamerica, of which I am the local administrator."

Downey gasped. Could it be that every one in the twenty-third century was mad?

"Well, are you going to speak or not?" piped the Councillor, leaning down from his throne until Downey thought he was about to fall off. "I'm giving you your chance to prove where you come from!"

As simply as he could, Downey attempted to state the facts of his origin; although he felt convinced that there would be little gain in arguing with a lunatic. And, as he foresaw, his words evoked only merriment. "Truly, stranger," said the chief tormentor, after he, the courtiers and the guards had all rocked back and forth with laughter, "you have little imagination, if you cannot think of a better story! So you were born in the year 1915! That is, 1915 by the old reckoning! Why, that would make you older than I! And I'm the most elderly man in this district, even though I won't celebrate my two hundred and seventy-fifth birthday till next year!"

Downey stared, and said nothing, more convinced than ever of the Councillor's madness.

"Of course, if it were not for you young man," the leader went on, meditatively, "I would have been in my grave two centuries ago. It is you who supply us with the robust young bodies to keep our old heads alive. I well remember how, just two hundred and nine years ago, I was pronounced at the point of death from heart disease—and the transfusion to a young body was performed barely in the nick of time. Since then, I've had the operation repeated once every thirty years—which accounts for my present good health."

From amid these rambling phrases, Downey had begun to catch a gleam of horrible meaning. Was the old man really mad after all? Or had he and his followers been kept alive through some dread process of grafting new bodies on to old heads?

Even as these questions flashed across the young man's mind, he heard the renewed rasping of the Councillor's voice, "I give you one final chance, sir! If you can't explain who you are and where you're from, you will be honored, according to the law of Nuamerica, by giving your head—"

He was interrupted by a half muffled cry. Judith, with one hand to her mouth, had vainly tried to keep back her horror.

The scowl on the Councillor's mummy face gave way to a faint smile as he turned to the girl, and said, "Have no fear, lady. You will not share in the honor. Don't you know that the Official Head Commission only last year exempted women from the Draft?"

"Have no fear, lady," the counsellor said, "you will not share the honor. You are exempt."

And then, blandly turning to the guards, the Councillor ordered, "Take the prisoners to the body-testing rooms. I believe we are up on our schedule, are we not?"

"Yes, Your Highness," returned the leader of the guards, bowing until his bare knees touched the floor, "there is no reason why your desires should not be executed within three days."

"Splendid!" approved the Councillor; while Downey, his arms still bound by the cramping wires, felt himself being drawn away in the midst of his grinning, kilted captors.

S tripped to the waist, Downey stood in a gray steel room that somewhat resembled the turret of a battleship. Gun-shaped implements bristled from the grim painted walls; a veritable arsenal of knives glistened behind him; while in the foreground was a series of tall machines equipped with an intricacy of dials and tubes, to one of which Downey's left arm had been strapped.

Just behind Downey stood a queer looking individual; robed in black, although with bare knees, according to the local custom; and with a black mask, and two tubes like doubly long opera glasses attached to his eyes. Eagerly he was bending over the dials, and reciting, half as though to himself, "339. 339.1. 340.1. 340.3." Then, with sudden enthusiasm, he snapped off the mask and glasses, revealing a wizened ancient face, and exclaimed,

"Young man, I congratulate you! You have passed!"

"Passed what, Doctor?" demanded Downey, as the examiner freed his arms from the straps.

"Passed the body test! You have come through with high honors! I never saw a more perfect physique! No flaw—no disease! Your score is more than three hundred and forty—and two hundred and thirty, as you may know, is considered a good average. I shall recommend you for immediate decapitation! My congratulations again, young man!"

Downey glared at the blacked robed one. "I don't know what you're talking about," he said. "It seems to me nearly every one here has lost his head, but that's no reason I want to lose mine!"

"Ah, but it's considered a glorious thing, young man! To be decapitated for your country's sake! Not every one can rise to such heights! Your name will be enshrined in the Tablet of Heroes!"

"I can get along without that," stated Downey, drily. "All I'm asking to know is what this nonsense is all about."

"Nonsense? You won't think it's nonsense, young man, when you put your neck under the knife!"

Noting the look of bewilderment and horror on Downey's face, the Doctor continued in a different vein:

"Well, maybe I'd better explain. I'm coming to see you're sincere in claiming ignorance. Not that I can accept that silly story about the twentieth century. But judging from your looks, your queer accent and out-of-date manners, you are undoubtedly from some foreign country, where maybe the people are uncivilized and don't know anything about decapitation."

The black-robed one seated himself on a little revolving stool, crossed his legs, and slowly went on:

"The original invention was made about three hundred years ago, by a physician named John Knight, who lived in an ancient city called New York. Was it necessary, Knight asked, for our best and most brilliant minds to be taken from us at the early age of seventy or eighty owing to some bodily defect? If fed by a vigorous blood-stream, the brain would continue to function indefinitely—perhaps for centuries. But a vigorous blood-stream, after senility had set in, could come only from another body. Therefore, Dr. Knight concluded, if an old man's head were grafted on to the body of a youth, the old man might continue to live, with new limbs and organs, but with mental faculties unimpaired. Think what a boon it would be for the race, if we could keep our great geniuses alive for hundreds of years!"

"But how was it possible, Doctor," broke in Downey, "to attach one man's body to another man's head?"

"It wasn't possible until after long experimentation. But the same principle had already been applied in the grafting of limbs. There was a gas, Etherene by name, which would produce suspended animation for a few hours, even stopping the heartbeat and the circulation of the blood. Any part of a man's body might be cut off while he was in this condition; and if ligament was fitted to ligament, bone to bone, and blood-vessel to blood-vessel, the removed portion might be attached in its proper place to the body of another Etherene patient. Of course, this required skilled surgery. But it was found that, by making proper measurements in advance, it was possible to graft arms, legs, ears, eyes and even whole bodies on to new possessors."

"That doesn't explain," remarked Downey, grimly, "where the new bodies would come from."

"No, it doesn't." The speaker arose, pointed to a crimson wall-chart marked, "Selective Decapitation Draft," and then went on to state, "There has been a great deal of trouble on that score. In fact, the Anti-Draft Revolution of the Twenties was fought on these grounds alone. First, as to whose lives would be preserved by the new invention. Of course, our rulers voted themselves that privilege. Also, the friends and relations of the rulers. Then all persons whose income tax was high enough were automatically entitled to remain alive. Furthermore, those who got in by what is vulgarly called graft—unfortunately, there have been some scandals on that account. And, finally, if there were bodies enough to go around, a place was to be made for the geniuses, such as great scientists, philosophers, poets, etc.

"I regret greatly to say, however," the Doctor concluded, with a sigh, "that we have never yet gotten that far down on the list."

"That still doesn't tell me," Downey insisted, "where you get the young bodies to attach to the old heads."

"Well, that has always been a problem," admitted the Doctor. "At first we used the bodies of criminals condemned to capital punishment. But the age was a humane one, and abolished capital punishment. Then we called for volunteers. But people showed a decided lack of patriotism. So finally we adopted the draft. All young men between twenty-one and thirty-one must be permanently registered. If they are selected in the great annual lottery and are found to be without taint or disease, they will have the blessed fate of giving their bodies to rejuvenate their country's aged leaders."

"But are the drafted men the only ones taken?" inquired Downey, anxiously.

"No, we are broad-minded. We offer the same distinguished lot to criminals—and to aliens without a passport. That is how you gained your chance, young man. As it happens, we are now far down the list. Your turn will come in just three days."

With a groan, Downey stared at the gray, knife-lined walls that hedged him about like a fortress prison. For the first time in his life he regretted—and bitterly regretted—the care he had always taken to keep in prime physical condition. He chewed his lips in mortification to think that he had come to the twenty-third century only in order to nourish some tottering dodo with his life blood. But for one reason above all others he was stabbed with grief: a vision had burst over him of Judith's eager face and burning bright blue eyes; and with a rush of vehement emotion it came to him that he could not, must not die! How would she fare, alone and friendless in this strange century? To escape from the bleak steel walls appeared impossible; yet for her sake, more than for his own, he must find a way to avert the threatened doom.

IV

Two days had gone by. Up and down the length of a long curtained room Downey slowly paced, with drooping head and drawn white face. Sumptuously upholstered chairs and carven tables were ranged about him, as if to lend luxury to his final hours. But it was not these that he observed; his eyes were drawn constantly to the door, which was crossed with steel bars, beyond which two kilted figures stood beside an ugly black apparatus resembling a machine-gun.

Bitterly he reviewed in his mind his fruitless efforts to free himself. The windows were locked and grated; the single door was guarded, and he was under constant surveillance. Every effort had been made to render his last days comfortable—but what comfort could he take when he was held like a doomed ox in the stall, awaiting the slaughter? He had hardly slept and barely taken food; and the final irony, he thought, occurred when he was handed a steel plaque which read, "The Purple Badge of Heroism. Died for his country this Thirty-Third day of May, in the year 314 of the New Era."

"Well, guess I'm as good as dead already," he reflected as he stared at these words.

He had flung the iron plaque to the furthest corner of the room, and had sunken into a chair with his head buried in his hands, when a rattling at the door caused him to start up abruptly.

"A visitor to see the prisoner!" he heard one of the guards droning, automatically. And the other responded, as automatically, "Let her in! Let her in!"

Leaping up, he observed Judith peering dismally through the bars.

"Mort!" she cried, in tones of mingled joy and sadness; while as he sprang forward to meet her he observed that two kilted women and a guard accompanied her. He also noted—and was a little hurt at the incongruity of the fact—that she had taken pains with her make-up: she was carrying her handbag, and the rouge on her lips was particularly thick, and the powder was smeared on her cheeks in great white patches.

"Mort, I—I've done everything," she exclaimed, as she flung out both hands to him. "But it was—it was no use. They wouldn't even let me see you till this minute. I—I've come to say good-bye, Mort."

He noticed that her big blue eyes were brimmed with tears. And in the tumult of that moment his own eyes were moist. With a swift impulse, he drew her to him, bending down and pressing his lips against hers. But, even as he did so, a powerful restraint seized him against his will. Caught by a sudden spasm, he turned aside, inwardly cursing—and sneezed.

Then again he sneezed, and again, and again, with fierce explosiveness; and the tears rolled from his eyes, which began to grow red and inflamed. Seven times in all he sneezed; then, with a growl, he muttered, "Damnation! There goes my hay-fever again!"

"Your what?" the guard inquired, not quite catching the words. "What kind of fever did you say?"

"Hay-fever," Judith answered. "It's a pestilence that used to rage in the twentieth century."

"Never heard of it," said the guard; at which the girl, drawing a mirror and powder-puff from her bag, began to smear her face anew; while Downey once more sneezed violently.

"Sounds mighty dangerous!" concluded the guard; and opening a little black tube on the wall, he called into it, "Send Doctor ZX down here at once! The prisoner has a fit!"

Downey was just completing his third sneezing spell a minute or two later when the black-robed Doctor arrived. With a dismayed gasp, he stared at Downey; then opened a little case and took out a mass of batteries and wires, which he attached to the prisoner's wrists and ankles, while he damped two tubes to his ears and listened.

While he was doing this, Judith was using her powder-puff again, and Downey once more sneezed.

"I don't know just what the disturbance is," the Doctor at length decided, gloomily. "There's some hidden functional derangement. The heartbeat is too fast. And the nerve pressure is too low. It's too bad, young man, that you should have to spoil a good record."

Downey's answer was to sneeze once more.

"I can't imagine what causes the fits," meditated the Doctor, while conducting a further examination. "It's something new to medical science. For all I know, it may be contagious. Worst of all the germs are probably in your body, and would infect any head to which you were attached."

"It was considered worse than smallpox in our own time," contributed Judith.

The Doctor paced slowly about the room, shaking his aged head doubtfully; while he himself, as Judith continued operation with the powder-puff, all at once began to sneeze.

"By my old head, I do hope I haven't caught it too!" he snapped, withdrawing from Downey anxiously. And then, with sudden decisiveness, "That settles it! I'm afraid I have bad news for you, young man. All our decapitation heroes, as you know, must be in the best physical condition. We can't take the chance of having them contaminate an old head. Our rule is, 'Safety first.' So you see, young man, I am left no choice. I will have to withdraw my recommendation!"

"What?" demanded Downey, rushing toward the Doctor in a wild outburst of joy. "Does that mean I won't be decapitated?"

"Keep away from me!" snarled the Doctor, making a dash toward the door. "Of course it means that! There's no use arguing, either! Henceforth you'll have to earn your living like any ordinary head-wearing citizen!"

As Judith's attendants and the guard withdrew, a startling thought burst over Downey.

"By heaven, Jude," he exclaimed, "how did I happen to get hay-fever already? My death-plaque said it's only May. And you know the fever season doesn't begin till August."

Judith looked up at him with streaming eyes in which a faint light was dawning. "Silly!" she said. "Why do you think I kept rubbing so much powder on my face? Don't you remember, you always used to complain, you were allergic to it, and it made you sneeze so much?"

"Well, thank the Lord for face powder!" cried the rescued man, as he suddenly realized how long and ingeniously the girl had been planning to save him—and realized, also, what such planning implied.

"It *is* lucky I brought my handbag with me from the twentieth century—and the face powder in it," stated the girl.

But his arms had already reached down to seize her. And, for the first time, she responded fully to his embrace.

"I—I—I didn't know how much I cared, Mort," she sobbed, "until I thought—I thought they were going to kill you!"

"Well, after all, decapitation has some merits," he smiled back. "Come to think of it, Jude, it doesn't matter much to me what century I'm in, so long as I'm there with you."